Other Kinds of Love:

A Short Story Collection

to Alejandra–
Enjoy!

STEPHANIE HADDAD

OTHER KINDS OF LOVE

TABLE OF CONTENTS

OTHER KINDS OF LOVE

INTRODUCTION

In my everyday life, I spend a lot of time thinking about what love is, what love means, and what love looks like. I'm a romance writer and a work-from-home mom. And as such, love is all around me, all the time. Love, in my life, has many faces.

Sometimes, it's the passionate first love scene between my two main characters. The riveting, ahem, climax that cements their relationship… at least until I try to pull them apart forever with an unexpected tragedy/secret past/misunderstanding. That kind of love is fun, because it all unfolds inside my head, where no one else can touch it.

But when I'm "in the trenches" of my life as a mother, love looks a little bit different. Sometimes, it's picking spaghetti out of my toddler's curly locks of hair, while counting to ten and replacing swear words with nonsense words like "cheese and rice" under my breath. Sometimes, love is bathing the dog, who clearly can't be trusted to perform this task herself.

Sometimes, love is greeting my husband at the door and asking him to spare me any further torture at the hands of these small monsters.

Love isn't always pretty or what we expected it to be. It's dirty, messy, dangerous, and downright unpredictable. And because I spend so much time writing the exact opposite of this in all of those romance novels, these short stories sprung to life in direct protest.

In the following pages, you'll read the stuff other romance writers don't write. There are no happily ever after ride into the sunset endings in this collection. Sorry. Instead, these stories are about other kinds of love—the stuff between families, strangers, and even people and their possessions.

Love's not perfect, but it's everywhere. I hope you'll see some of the love in your life reflected in these pages.

Happy reading!

xx Stephanie Haddad xx

TO KILL A SPIDER

They both stared at the white wall, just under the molding where the ceiling paint had begun to chip from water damage. "It's right there, can't you see it?" Lauren spoke, pointing vigorously toward the tiny, nearly invisible entity.

"Are you sure?"

"Would you just listen to me? I know what it is, so just get a chair and some paper towels already!"

As Steve turned toward the kitchen to retrieve his necessary effects, he mumbled to himself something that sounded quite unkind toward his wife.

In her early childhood, Lauren had developed and refined a kind of spider-radar. What others would take for a mere speck of dust, Lauren would correctly identify as a spider from a room's length away. This was surprising to friends and family, as Lauren's eyesight with respect to other distant objects—especially road signs—was poor at best. Those around her, when such a sighting took place, often doubted her; confirmation of the invader could only be made with the assistance of a chair or step-ladder in extreme close proximity. Lauren herself would avoid such a proximity at all costs; thus giving rise to the now infamous tennis shoe tossing incident that claimed the life of one passing arachnid back in 1992.

Her sighting accuracy was both impressive and irritating to Steve; would it really matter if one of the little creatures got away unscathed? Undoubtedly yes, Lauren would argue. Such an intruder was to receive the ultimate in cruel punishments: a fatal dousing of Dow bathroom cleaner and a paper towel. If the spider was small and less threatening, Lauren granted it a merciless execution by shoe sole or squishing in a Kleenex. But her rule was firm; none shall cross her line of sight and live to tell the tale. And of course, as Lauren was queen of her surroundings, all treasonous offenders would be dealt with by her beloved husband Steve, the loyal executioner. This had been the law of the land for some years now.

Lauren stood, tapping her foot impatiently, with her arms crossed and her eyes fixed on the spider. She was used to Steve resisting her demands, but this time he seemed to be taking much longer than usual. Feeling confident that the little creature could not possibly descend three feet and viciously attack her within five seconds' time, she allowed herself to break her gaze. She looked toward the kitchen for Steve, who stood in the doorway with a kitchen chair and a roll of white paper towels.

"Aren't you going to get up there and kill it?" she hissed, growing nervous with every extra second of life the spider was granted. Steve stood still, a troubled look on his face. "What's the matter?"

"Well, I was just standing here, thinking. I've never really given much thought to the implications of killing spiders. I'm not really sure that I want to do this, ya know? It's just that…"

"What?!"

"Who says we have the right to kill them all?"

"The *right?*" Lauren spat the word at him. "Are you insane? It's a spider!"

"Exactly. It's a living, breathing, thinking being."

"Spiders don't think, Steve."

"How do you know? They can respond to predators and prey, they have instincts that protect them and keep them alive. That sounds like thinking to me."

"Acting on instinct is much different from thinking. Spiders have instincts."

"That were programmed by God."

"What?!" This nonsense was wasting precious time. There should be a spider carcass in the trash by now. "What are you talking about?"

"Well, in the Bible…"

"Steve, you don't even like the Bible."

"Yes, but most people do. You sorta do, don't you?" He looked to Lauren for confirmation and received nothing but a laser stare that could rival Superman's. "Well anyway, in the Bible it says that God created all creatures. Shouldn't you be more sensitive to the lowly ones?"

"If you'd continued reading, you'd have learned that God also created man to rule over the other creatures. Honestly, Steve, if you're going to start putting stock into the Bible now, you have to take the whole text together. You can't just pick out the parts you like and use those to back up your argument."

"Why not? That's what they do with statistics." Steve, gaining confidence by the minute, relaxed onto the kitchen chair with his arms crossed and the paper towels resting across his lap. He had Lauren's full attention now; she hadn't looked up for the spider in almost four full minutes. "For example, did you ever hear the statistic that you swallow eight spiders a year while you're sleeping?"

Lauren gagged audibly.

"It's probably true, but they fail to mention how many other bugs you probably swallow in a year. Spiders might not even be the most popular choice for late-night insect snacking. They chose that stat to launch an entire slander campaign against spiders."

"Slander?" Lauren slumped into the battered, second-hand recliner and cradled her swimming head in her hands.

"Yes, Lauren. Mankind has painted a picture of spiders as lesser-beings, who should be subjugated and slaughtered. It's wrong, just wrong." He stood up dramatically, and the paper towels fell from his lap and unrolled across the blue shag carpeting. "Spiders are helpful and necessary creatures!"

"Exactly how is terrifying the living daylights out of me a helpful skill?"

"Not that. It has nothing to do with you. It's so much bigger than that. They are a key link in the food chain, Lauren. They eat all those little annoying insects who..."

"Are far less menacing?"

"I think you've just got a bad attitude toward spiders," he said, his tone lightening as he knelt in front of her. "You just need to understand that finding one inside our house does not give us the right to sentence it to death."

It was Lauren's turn to rise dramatically, knocking Steve backward onto the blue shag carpeting. "You traitor!" she shrieked, a little too loudly. Checking herself, she continued more calmly. "I am your wife and you are supposed to protect me!"

"Honey, if I honestly thought you were in grave danger...."

"Like, if it was an invasion of 10-foot tarantulas?" she offered.

"Uh....sure. If a 10-foot tarantula, even a singular one, came after you King Kong style, then I would have something to say about it. But this little guy," he gestured toward the eight-legged offender, "He couldn't hurt a–"

"Oh yes, he could hurt a fly!"

"Sorry, wrong choice of phrasing. He *could* hurt a fly, sure, but is he really interested in hurting us?"

"Probably not..." Lauren admitted with difficulty.

"Then I really don't want to hurt him either."

Lauren drew in a breath, hesitating. She studied Steve's expression, looking for any sign that he was full of it. Nothing. "I guess I didn't realize how passionate you were about this. I don't really have anything to say to that."

"Thank you."

"So I guess I'll just head to bed. Are you coming? It's already after 11:00." She crossed the living room and headed for the bathroom. Steve could hear the water turn on as Lauren brushed her teeth.

Steve took a deep breath. "Sweet victory," he muttered to himself. "Live another day, little guy." He winked at the spider, now nestled cozily into the east corner of the ceiling, and followed Lauren to bed.

LIFE IN A BAG

Alice's life was in her purse, and sometimes the sheer magnitude of the clutter necessitated that she cleaned it out and started over. After six months of filling the pockets with odds and ends, the bag had grown so heavy that she could hardly lift it anymore. It was time for a clean slate, so today was cleaning day. Alice vigorously shook the eclectic contents onto the table in a muddled heap that slowly spread in every direction; colorful tubes of lipstick rolled off the table's edge and crumpled receipts fluttered to the floor. Heaving a sigh, she set about the bi-annual task with little enthusiasm.

The usual suspects were present and accounted for: the key ring overloaded with those belonging to old apartments that Alice no longer inhabited; the battered Coach wallet with the fraying corners, stuffed to the brim with plastic cards and coinage; the reading glasses she never wore, tucked safely inside their quilted case; the sunglasses she hadn't required since the last time she'd cleaned out her purse; and the pair of leather gloves she'd gotten this

Christmas that had already saved her freezing fingers on numerous occasions. These things she extracted delicately from the mountainous pile and set off to the side. Now, able to focus on the minutiae, Alice began sorting the clutter into categories.

Six tubes of lipstick. Three of which were the same color, a deep russet red that made her lips sultry and seductive. Two tubes were worn down to the tiniest nub, evidently used to excess during her fling with Richard, who said the lipstick made him horny. Alice selected a tube of pale plum from among the six and threw away the others.

Four nail files of different shapes, sizes and colors. Undoubtedly, these were leftover from a brief foray with acrylic fingernails that William had found to be too 'hooker-like' for his bland tastes. The filing had helped, but not enough, and eventually the nails had to go. She threw the files away, reconsidered, and kept the smallest one just in case.

Her failed GMAT test scores. Patrick had promised he'd help her to pass and they'd go to graduate school together. He'd lied. Trash.

Thirty-two assorted receipts from a variety of retailers, fast food peddlers, and ATM branches. Alice wondered why she always requested a receipt if she just left them to litter her bag until cleaning day, when they inevitably made it into the trash. Must've been a habit she picked up from Paul. These receipts met a waste-basket fate as Alice promised that her new bag would be a more eco-friendly version of its former self.

A bottle of separated, neon-green nail polish from Halloween. Gary had expressed a longing for hot women in witch's hats. Consequently, he'd also stood her up for a blond in a cat suit. Trash.

The pearl earrings from Steve. They looked expensive. Trash? No, sell them.

Two checkbooks, one for each bank account, that hadn't been used in over a year. Alice never wrote checks and yet, the thought of leaving the house without them made her nervous. What if her bank card didn't work and it was an emergency? She remembered all too well that night she got stranded in Pittsburgh with Geoff. Feeling somewhat justified by this rationale, Alice decided that even new things could retain old habits and decided to keep the checkbooks.

A small army of loose buttons, most of which probably didn't even belong to Alice's garments. Again, she blamed Paul's pack-rat tendencies. Since she'd lost touch with many of their male owners, Alice decided not to keep them. With one sweep of her arm across the table, they bounced unceremoniously into the trash barrel.

The lint roller she'd bought three months ago, a precautionary measure to protect her Ann Taylor pant suits from Eric's shedding shih tzu. She didn't need it anymore, but reasoned that it may come in handy in other non-dog-related situations. Alice tucked it into the outer pocket.

Finally, a solitary brass key was all that remained on the table. It wasn't hers. Alice tried to remember who had given her the key, and for what purpose. She had probably been meant to return it, but it seemed too late for that now if she couldn't even recall what it unlocked. Convinced she'd never need it, but unwilling to admit that she might never see its owner again, Alice hid the key in a tiny interior pocket. She had a feeling she'd done this several times before, at other cleanings, but couldn't say how long she'd had the key. Still, hope prevailed and the key remained. Just in case.

And then, with her new bag and her new life freed from the remnants of Richard, William, Paul, Patrick, Gary, Steve, Geoff and Eric, Alice headed out the door. It was another day in her eternal search for one man who could fill her entire purse, not just a tiny interior pocket.

COUNTER PRODUCTIVE

I hate people that look into this mirror as if no one else can see them. They check their teeth, pucker their lips (how's this lipstick?), fuss with their hair, suck in their stomach, turn sideways (how's my stomach from this side?), and look ridiculous. But it's ok, because they don't know that other people are watching. Ah, sweet obliviousness.

This particular mirror gets a lot of action. It's situated in a central location, in the midst of a department-like store that isn't quite sure what it wants to be when it grows up. *Are we a clothing retailer? How about a bookseller? No, I got it, we sell souvenirs! How about we just sell everything?* And that is how this mirror ended up amongst this conglomerate of merchandise, proudly affixed to the front right corner of our makeup counter.

My job is to watch these people watch themselves in the mirror. My job is also to tell these people, harshly critiquing themselves in my mirror, what they can buy that will make them like themselves, if not completely, then at least more than they do now. Sell them whatever that is and all of its accessories.

My boss calls me a 'drug-dealer' because of my ruthless targeting of these self-loathers.

"Just try this *one thing* and I'll give you free samples of some other amazing products that you can come back to buy later. You'll love them. I promise."

And I do this and they come back. Now they're hooked. Now they trust me and they trust this brand that I mercilessly sell to them. And above all, now I can make my commission.

Lipstick is the gateway drug. We find the perfect lipstick that completes you; it makes you the woman you want to be.

"It brightens your face, compliments your hair color and really brings out your eyes. Perfect. This color, I do believe, was manufactured simply for you. Buy it. Wear it. Love it."

Sadly, your glorious lipstick-to-end-all-lipsticks is *just slightly* wrong for your eye shadow. Don't have a complimentary color at home?

"That's ok, we have them here! Lots of them; you can buy them in sets. Here's a great daytime color, and this shade will be perfect for evening wear. Oh yes, of course, you're going to need this sexy, sultry new eyeliner we just debuted (three years ago). Don't even get me going on that horrible drug-store mascara you're wearing that's most definitely filled with bacteria. Mother of God, how can you do this to yourself?"

And that cheek color you have on is clearly a pink tone. Hello, 1985? That just won't do if you're wearing this violet-toned lipstick day-in and day-out.

"Here, this is better. And just apply it like so, with this *special* $30 blush brush with handcrafted bristles by community-trade African workers in Zambia. It's 100% synthetic. And so soft. Isn't that something?"

Now you're in. If you stay in my chair long enough, you can leave with a brand new face. None of your friends will believe it. You'll be gorgeous. You might even get promoted or get a hot date tonight.

"Take a chance, live a little. You deserve it."

I hate mirrors. I especially hate *this* mirror because it makes me do this to innocent passers-by who are careless with their wallets. If only they knew that I was watching, maybe they wouldn't have made such a fuss in the mirror. Vulnerability is my appetizer and your wallet is my entree. And I hate that I find it so delicious.

NANA'S AID

Squeezed snuggly into the pew between my theologically enraptured mother and despondent teenage brother, I willed myself not to fall asleep during Easter mass. I feared that if I did, I'd most surely be snoring within five minutes, especially after the long day's travel from New York to Boston that I had just endured. It would have been nice if I'd at least had time to change out of my leather pants before attending a public worship service.

The priest's familiar voice rang throughout the church, delivering a speech in equal length to the Gettysburg Address, and almost as interesting. As he droned on, I could feel myself slipping. Father John, most fortuitously, raised his voice in an echoing crescendo to proclaim 'eternal damnation lest ye fight temptation by the devil,' or something like that. In any case, it was enough to set off Nana's ultrasensitive hearing aid. The whirring, bleating noise successfully jarred me from my peaceful thoughts of slumber.

"Alright, alright," she shrieked, banging the heel of her palm against the side of her head. "Damned thing. Shut up already!"

At this, even my younger brother, who had been previously engrossed in the conquest of another level of game play on his Nintendo DS, looked over at my beloved Nana. Evidently, family mockery was just a nudge more exciting than slaying dragons. He rolled his eyes at me before returning to his game.

I realized that the priest had actually paused and the whole congregation sat unmoving, collectively holding their breath. My mother was frozen with embarrassment, which was par for the course when my family traveled anywhere en masse.

Suddenly, I saw my salvation.

"Come on, Nana, I'll help you," I whispered, stepping over my twitching mother and ushering my grandmother toward the exit.

"WHAT? Can't hear you! This thing won't stop beeping in my ear," Nana replied, endearingly. Regardless, she followed me to the back of the church and outside into the crisp spring air. The side of her head bleared impatiently while we walked, as I ground my teeth just to bear the sound. Seeing as I'd just completed a three-year stint of orthodontist care, I decided I'd better put an end to this quickly.

As the door closed behind us, I could almost hear the congregation's collective sigh of relief. I sighed with relief too.

Reluctantly, my grandmother placed her malfunctioning octogenarian accessory into my outstretched hand. I silently thanked my mother for teaching me how to shut such devices off at the age of 11. In the fifteen years that my grandmother had been wearing this healthcare scam of a device, it had probably worked well for about five of them. The rest of the time it just made enough noise that no one could hear anything else, especially my grandmother.

When the noise cut off abruptly, I relaxed my clenched jaw completely and handed the hearing aid back to my grandmother. "Here you go, Nana."

"Thanks, sweetheart. Now, what were we up to?" She stared at me blankly, head cocked to one side and hearing aid still in hand.

"Nana, you need to put your hearing aid back in," I said politely.

"Yes, OK," she did as instructed and then looked back at me for approval.

"OK, Nana, we have to go back in," I turned toward the large double doors tightly shut behind us. "Come on."

"Oh, I love Mass," Nana began excitedly. "Is there a pageant today? I hope there's a pageant. When I was a girl, I played one of the three wisemen in a pageant. Are you going to be in it?"

"The Mass?"

"No, the pageant!"

"Nana, there's no pageant today,"

"Well, when I was a girl…" she began again.

"I know. You were one of the three wisemen," I interrupted sharply. "But that's at Christmas. It's Easter."

"That is not what I was going to say," she retorted indignantly. I suddenly felt guilty for losing patience with my dear, aging grandmother. It's true that her dementia was, at times, a challenge to deal with, but I had no excuse to be rude to her. "Now, tell me. Why are we standing in front of a church?"

"Mass, Nana," I spoke quietly, swallowing hard.

"So, sweetheart," Nana said kindly, her attentions drawn downward to my embarrassing wardrobe choice. She pointed to the black leather, glistening in the sunlight. "Are we going to a big party somewhere? I can bring some petit fours with us and maybe we can pick up some Madagascar Vanilla Beans to put on top."

"No, Nana," I explained. "I sing with a band in New York City. I came home on the bus overnight and I didn't have time to change."

"I like them," she said cheerfully, smiling at me. "Did you come back to visit me?"

"Yes, for Easter," I said again. Conversation with Nana was sometimes like beating my head against a brick wall. Seeing as she used to be my primary confidant, even outranking my mother, I couldn't stand to see her this way. I felt like I'd lost a trusted friend.

"Where's Joe?" she asked innocently, oblivious to my downcast expression.

I cringed, stiffening at his name. Now, I longed to be sitting in that church pew again, blessed with silent solitude.

"We don't see each other anymore," came my automated reply. In fact, we hadn't seen each other in three very long, very painful years. I couldn't blame Nana, but it didn't help me that she kept asking for him every time I saw her.

Just as I was thinking that my Nana was completely lost to me, she said exactly what I needed to hear, reminding me how deeply we were still connected.

"Well then, Patty, you've gotta get back out there in those leather pants and meet another nice boy. You can do better than Joe," she beamed as she hugged me tightly. My eyes brimmed with tears. "Now, what are we standing out here for?"

HIS LETTER

For seven years, his letter lay nestled behind the mantelpiece, a silent witness to Rachel's lonely journey. She didn't know it was there; she couldn't possibly know. He'd left it propped up against an old snow globe without a word, trusting she would find it but unable to stay any longer and be sure. Then he'd left Rachel, out of necessity, all those years ago.

When his letter had first slid into its snug, unseen slot between the mantle and the wall, blown there by a fated gust of wind, it had remained optimistic. It had waited and waited, ever patient and hopeful. Rachel would find it. One day, she would see its white, crisp corner poking from between the drywall and stone; she *had* to see it.

But days became weeks and nothing changed. Except for Rachel. His letter heard her crying in lonely agony during the night. It ached to comfort her, as he would have done if he were still here. And it could bring her that comfort. His letter held all the answers—why he had left, where he would meet her again, how much he loved her. Rachel, knowing no explanation, needed to find it. Still, his letter could do nothing but listen.

As weeks became months, the spring breeze warmed to a sweltering heat, and still the letter waited. Eventually, Rachel's sobbing lessened. More time passed between her bouts of sadness, like slowing thunderclaps as a storm passes overhead. Laughter replaced bitter sobbing; new voices—sometimes male—echoed in her tiny home, reverberating off the walls and shaking his letter's wilting envelope.

In turn, his letter grew accustomed to its neglect and learned to appreciate its darkened surroundings. It befriended the graying cobwebs and dust bunnies, the pieces of cracked plaster that had fallen from the wall, and the long-lost buttons and threads doomed to this secret cranny of the house.

Over the years, one male voice became constant, laughing and talking with Rachel for long hours into the night. This man said the things that *he* would have said to her. His letter, still harboring those loving words she had never read, began to lose hope. It knew she might never find it now; her life was moving forward without him. The letter would lay here in wait until time destroyed it.

But the letter knew that his one wish was for Rachel to be happy. He might never know she hadn't read it; he might think she'd chosen to forget him. The letter knew that they would both live on in each other's hearts, but the path between them was forever lost.

THE CAN MAN

The clattering metal rings in your ears before you see anything. It clangs, rattles, rolls toward you in a dizzying whirr of sound. It draws closer, just as it has every morning before today, the rustling plastic bags sliding back and forth along the bottom of the criss-crossed metal. The cans and bottles inside the shopping cart jostle with every crack in the weather-beaten sidewalk. He's getting closer and soon you'll get a glimpse. Maybe even a whiff.

Automatically, your eyes focus toward the sound, until a blur of red and black plaid flannel emerges around the corner. The short, stocky figure teeters back and forth, edging the noisy shopping cart toward your frozen stance at the bus stop. Is he cold today too? No hat, no gloves. Only a thin layer of flannel shields his skin from the bitter wind chill. But he beams ear-to-ear, smiling as he passes squirrels and trees, ignoring the honking cars of the Monday morning road, as though cold could not damper his mood.

Just a few feet away now. His heavy cologne catches on the breeze and lingers in the air around you. The sticky smells of cola and stale beer waft upward from today's collection of recyclables. The cart announces his arrival with a metallic smash as it moves over a tree root. His smile finds you now, too late for you to look away today, and he gives you the same enthusiasm shown to the little pieces of nature along his route.

"Hi." He pauses in front of you, his worn gloves wrapped around the handle of the cart. He's done this every day and yet his expression betrays no recognition. You are as new a discovery to him as every collected can. He longs to collect a smile from you today, like every day, and you plan to deny him again.

But the whipping wind and the frozen ground beneath your feet suddenly disappear with the warmth of his smile.

"Hi." The word escapes your sore, chapped lips before you've thought to speak it. You smile, the corners of your cracked mouth stretching uncomfortably. The pain makes you flinch and your smile evaporates. But it's enough.

He stops for a moment, nods his thanks, and then resumes. The clattering metal moves to the pace of his cheerful whistling and the can man continues his never-ending quest for forgotten recyclables and momentary companions.

UNGIFTABLE

"Only one gift left," Shirley said to her husband of six hours. Discarded bows, ribbons, and paper in various shades of wedding pastels surrounded them on the luscious duvet of their hotel bed. They'd promised to wait to open the gifts until the next day, but Shirley couldn't resist the call of their ornate paper. Wayne had put up limited resistance, finding his new wife too adorable to dissuade.

"Thank God for that," he said, brushing the torn wrappings onto the floor. He passed her the shimmering blue package. "Let's see what my old Aunt Gertie got for us, shall we?"

Shirley's hopes weren't high, not with Aunt Gertie's track record for giving expensive and tasteless gifts. Even so, when she tore away the delicate paper and popped open the nondescript brown box, she was still disappointed.

"How…unusual," she said kindly, tipping the box for her husband to see. He grunted in response, stifling his laughter. "What?"

"You don't have to be nice," Wayne said. He slid the box from the bed and his arm around his wife. "She's your aunt now, too."

After the honeymoon, Shirley tried to find a place for the little knick-knack. She thought it might be a collectible of some kind, possibly with some hidden value, so she vowed to keep it safe. When several valiant attempts were made to place the gift everywhere from the mantle to the bathroom with no success, Shirley gave up. Eventually, she wrapped it back in the box and banished it to the closet of an extra bedroom.

Some months later, Shirley and Wayne discovered that they would soon become the proud parents of a new baby girl. As so often happens, Shirley's motherly instincts spurred her to clean out the extra bedroom and redecorate it as a nursery. When she made it to the closet, she chuckled at the sight of the gift, resting forgotten in the corner beneath a shopping bag filled with unwanted clothing. As sudden inspiration struck her, Shirley took a gift bag from her own bridal shower, wrapped the gift snuggly in tissue paper, and tucked it inside.

That weekend, she brought it to a co-worker's wedding, abandoning it on a table brimming with other eccentrically adorned packages. Wayne and Shirley hoped the new couple would find a use for the gift.

It was several days before the Walters found the time to wade through the mountainous pile of gifts and compose their Thank You cards. Starting with non-family presents, Thomas selected an ivory gift bag while Rebecca aimed pen at paper.

"From the McIntyres," he announced to his wife. She started writing: *Dear Shirley and Wayne, Thank you so very much for...*

"Go ahead, open it," Rebecca said when she was ready.

Thomas slid the gift from the bag, unrolling the tightly wrapped tissue paper until he reached the center of its protective cocoon. But this was no butterfly. He hesitated a moment, scrunching up his nose in distaste, and then held it out for his wife to see.

"What is it?" she asked, pen still hovering. *Thank you so very much for the...* "Do you think it's a vase? Or a fish bowl?"

"Could be an ashtray," Thomas shrugged.

"Shirley knows we don't smoke." Rebecca took the gift from her husband and turned it over in her hands. It was delicate, fragile, and a vibrant shade of blue that wouldn't coordinate with a single thing in their home. "Huh. Made in China."

"Is that an elephant?"

"Come on, Tom," she laughed. "Be serious. What am I supposed to write? *Thank you so very much for the unidentifiable object that we will promptly place in the attic.*"

"How about we just say *your thoughtful gift*?" Thomas reached out and grabbed the next gift, eager to open something less puzzling and possibly from their registry.

The gift did, indeed, find a home in the attic. It stayed there for months, then years, as the Walters family lived their lives beneath it. A son was born, then a daughter.

Thomas contracted someone to build a new deck, then an addition on the back. Eventually one day, Rebecca ventured into the depths of the attic, humming to herself as she organized four years' worth of collected junk.

"Oh, look at this," she said, grasping the gift with two hands. "I remember you. And I think it might be time for a change of scenery, whatever you are. Let's get you some shiny red paper and I'll take you to a party."

Rebecca Walters wrapped the gift once more, this time in festive Christmas paper, and brought it to her neighbor's Yankee Swap. Jean, the hostess, had suggested everyone bring something unwanted from their own home. Rebecca thought this gift was perfect.

Unfortunately, Suzy Fitzgibbon did not agree. Attracted by the gleaming paper, Suzy selected it from the gift pile and eagerly tore it open. Instantly, her face contorted with disappointment and confusion.

"What is that?" Jean laughed from across the room, clutching a pair of snowman-shaped salt and pepper shakers. Suzy had been hoping for something cute and innocuous like those or even the remote control caddy that Louisa Jones had opened. Instead she was stuck with this, a poorly-constructed excuse for kitsch.

"Now remember, Suzy," teased Rebecca. "You have to take home what you open!"

No one swapped gifts with her, though Suzy made every effort to negotiate, even offering free snow-shoveling if someone would take that *thing* off her hands. When the party ended, she took it home and assigned it a dark corner of the garage.

The Fitzgibbon's garage had a leak they did not know about, and as the seasons changed, the gift suffered a handful of hurricane seasons and a dozen blizzards. The boxes around it began to mildew. Several generations of spiders and insects crawled across the gift, never stopping to consider using it as a home. Even the raccoons that broke in one fall, before getting chased out by Suzy's husband Ralph and a broom, never gave the gift a second look. Utterly forlorn, it seemed the gift was condemned to a life of forgotten solitude.

And then Ralph's company decided to transfer him overseas. The Fitzgibbon family sprung into action, cleaning, organizing and packing. To cover the moving expenses, Suzy and Ralph decided to hold a yard sale and the whole family soon set about the arduous task of clearing out the garage.

"What on earth is this?" Little Janie cried at the sight of the gift. She picked it up with two fingers, blowing off the dust and cobwebs. "Where did it come from?"

Suzy shooed her away, took the item from her hands and placed it in the SELL pile. "It was a gift."

"It's ugly," Janie stuck out her tongue. "I don't think anyone will buy that, Mom."

Two weeks later, their yard sale made them over $1000 in profits. Suzy sold most of their furniture, several boxes filled with old baby clothes and toys, some old 45 records, and lots of assorted junk. Yet there, on a small table of leftovers, sat the gift—dusty, overlooked, and unloved. Suzy threw the leftovers into an empty box on the curb for trash pick-up the next morning. She tossed the gift inside carelessly, nearly breaking its fragile glass handle.

As Suzy cleared the trash and clutter from the yard, a woman and her daughter pulled up in front of the house. They got out of the car and began rifling through the mountain of unsold goods, studying the graying stuffed animals and beaten paperbacks with intent. Suddenly, the young girl shrieked with delight, plunging her hands into the bottom of the box.

"I love it!" she exclaimed, extracting the gift from the rubble. Smiling, she turned to her mother, who gazed back at the gift in shocked disbelief. The light refracted through the blue glass and painted a rainbow across the pavement. "May I keep it, Mommy?"

Suzy nodded to the mother, who then smiled at her daughter.

"Yes, Molly. Say thank you to the nice lady," she said. She didn't want it, but when Shirley McIntyre saw the happiness in her young daughter's eyes, she knew she'd never dissuade her. And how Wayne would laugh when he laid eyes on their discovery! At least now, after all these years, Shirley knew it would have a place in their home.

Someone finally wanted the gift.

A SMILE

Becca sat at her desk, kicking the legs of her plastic chair and twirling her pigtail. She stared out the classroom windows at the early September scene: a gaggle of geese flying over the red and orange treetops and the playground of her brand new school. Becca preferred to be playing outside so she could swing high above the school and catch one of those geese. Maybe Mom would let her keep it as a pet.

"Rebecca, are you paying attention?" Mrs. Carl tapped her foot impatiently. Becca whipped her head around, and could hear the other children in her class snickering. She kept her eyes forward, willing her scarlet face to cool down.

Becca mumbled an apology and sunk into her chair, longing to melt into a puddle under her desk. Panicked that the other kids were still laughing, Becca took a peek over her shoulder and saw a little blond boy. Accidentally making eye contact, she blushed again when a toothy smile crept across his face. A smile for her!

She wasn't quite sure what to do. She'd never met any boys before, except for her little brother Timmy. And this particular boy was much better looking than Timmy. Plus, he was probably potty-trained. He wore a white collared shirt and a clip-on tie, decorated with the Backyardigans, Becca's favorite show. She couldn't wait to tell him how much they had in common, because then they could be friends!

Becca knew her face was as red as that shiny car in the garage that Daddy doesn't drive, but she couldn't look away. The cute boy still was smiling at her, and waving too. Amazed, Becca flashed a nervous smile and whipped her head back around.

Wow! Becca had never had any friends before because she didn't know anyone her age. Imaginary friends didn't count. Mom said school was perfect for making friends and she was right.

Becca daydreamed straight through about a lesson on colors and shapes. At snack time, she opened her flip-top desk and pulled out her new Dora the Explorer lunch box. Inside it was a shiny red apple, some cheese and crackers and a bright purple juice box. Mmm… grape juice was her favorite. Mom was really good at packing snacks. Becca wondered what her Grandma had given her Mom for a snack on the first day of school.

Becca scanned the room, noticing thae other kids gathering into little groups on the floor. In fact, Becca was the only one sitting alone, until another little girl came over to her desk.

"Hi!" said the little brown-haired girl, smiling a huge grin that stretched the freckles on her cheeks.

"Hi," Becca replied, not sure what to say to make friends.

"My name's Kylie."

"I'm Becca." It was a good place to start.

"Do you want to sit with me for snack?"

That made two people who had made friends with Becca today, and she hadn't even done anything at all. She nodded enthusiastically at her new friend Kylie and followed her to a pile of naptime mats in the corner. Kylie spun around like a ballerina and plopped down on the mats. Becca took a seat next to her, without spinning, and noticed an identical lunchbox on her friend's lap.

Becca showed her. "Look, we have the same lunchbox!"

"Cool! That means we have to be friends!" Kylie giggled as she spoke. Becca couldn't agree more.

For the first few moments, they sat munching on apples and carrot sticks in an awkward silence. When Kylie finally spoke up, it startled Becca.

"So, how old are you? Is that your real name or is it short for something else? What's your favorite color? Do you like broccoli?" Kylie batted her eyelashes, waiting for an answer. Becca wasn't sure where to start

"I'm five," she started.

"Me too!" Kylie exclaimed, jumping up and knocking her juice box to the floor. "Oops!"

With Kylie distracted by spouting juice, Becca hurried to answer the other questions. "My name's Rebecca, but I like Becca better. My little brother can't say my name so he calls me Becca."

"You have a brother? Cool!" Kylie was hanging on every word Becca said, her eyes widening.

"You can meet him sometime." Becca was a little confused, but realized that she liked the attention. As excited as she was, though, Becca couldn't devote her full attention to Kylie. Every few minutes, she stole a glance across the room at the blond-haired boy, sitting on a pile of mats with a little girl in a pink dress and sharing snacks. Becca really wanted to move towards them, but Kylie wouldn't stop talking.

Soon, Mrs. Carl called the class back to learn numbers. All of this learning bothered Becca. She sighed as she packed up her lunchbox and returned to her seat, which happened to be the one behind Kylie.

Becca sat with her hands folded, giving her full attention to Mrs. Carl, but numbers were too boring. She couldn't help but glance outside again, where the wind was blowing the fallen leaves around the empty playground and the rain poured in a steady stream. Mom definitely wouldn't let Becca stay after school to play on the slide now.

The rain made numbers seem more exciting by comparison, so Becca turned back to the giant flashcards and tried to get interested. She even raised her hand to identify the number "2" and won a smile from Mrs. Car, who said, "Very good, Rebecca." Satisfied, Becca wanted to see what the little blond boy thought about how smart she was, so she turned around.

Sure enough, he was smiling at her. Becca realized that he hadn't answered any questions yet, so maybe they could be friends so she could teach him about numbers. She smiled back at him, accepting his offer of friendship.

Again he waved back, but this time, his glance seemed to go straight through Becca and a little to the right. Confused, she turned around in her seat, thinking someone might be outside the window, waving and smiling back at the little blond boy.

It was worse than that. Sitting there and smiling back was the little girl in the pink dress, blushing violently. Becca's heart sank; the boy had never wanted to be friends with her after all. She felt ridiculous as her face reddened for the first time in hours. Becca had really thought he liked her; in fact, she had really started to like him too.

Determined, Becca straightened in her chair, facing Kylie's ponytail. She considered answering all the questions to prove she was smarter than the other girl. She thought about wearing a little pink dress tomorrow and putting her mat next to his for naptime. Becca even thought about introducing herself to him after school.

Instead, she decided to mind her own business and forget about the flirtatious grins traveling through her oblivious pigtails. Maybe boys were too hard to make friends with just yet. For now, Becca decided to make Kylie her best friend, especially since Dora was better than the Backyardigans anyway. Her mind made up, she would switch seats tomorrow.

ONLY MOMENTS

I'm sitting on a couch, clutching an afghan like the ones I used to knit on my chest. There's a Band-Aid on one of my fingers. I don't know why, but it hurts if I squeeze it. Bing Crosby is singing on the TV in black and white. I sing along to myself, surprised to find I know all the words.

A young girl arrives. Her nose is like mine, her eyes seem familiar. I know I have known her for a long time, because my heart warms to see her face. I am smiling.

"Grandma," she greets me, and I keep smiling even though the name shakes me up a bit. "It's Jenny."

"I know that."

She smiles kindly, accepting my lie. "It's good to see you." When she hugs me, I feel smaller than I used to. I want to put this together into a thought, into a shared memory that will make us laugh.

"You're bigger." These are the only words I can find, but I wince at their wrongness.

"Yes." Her smile falters. "Still a few pounds to lose." I expect she might be mad, but she isn't. The girl—I've forgotten her name—takes my hand. I feel safe with her, so I follow.

#

I'm holding a baby I don't recognize. A young girl with a nose like mine, whose name dances on the tip of my tongue, talks to me in short sentences about this baby.

She stops when I look up at her. I have to ask. "Whose baby is this?"

"Mine, Grandma," the girl smiles and I think she looks like me when I had my baby. She looks tired, but happy, and still carries a little pudge around her middle. I won't say anything about that; I remember how upset I was when the pudge wouldn't go away. But this baby is not my baby, it's hers I know, but the baby feels solid in my arms, warm and soft. This baby sits on my lap and stares at me, reaching one hand up to my mouth.

I'm suddenly struck by something powerful. "She's so beautiful, Jenny. Just like you were." I say the words without trying and each syllable feels right on my lips. This is my precious Jenny and her perfect angel baby.

I look at the girl again, who wipes a tear away with one knuckle, and I have a thought. Tissues. I used to keep them tucked in my sleep. Does she need a tissue? I could get her one—

"Grandma?"

A little hand grabs mine. I look at the baby, then at the young girl. "Whose baby is this?" I ask.

#

"Mary?"

I'm sitting on a couch, clutching an afghan like the ones I used to knit on my chest. There's a Band-Aid on one of my fingers. I don't know why, but it hurts if I squeeze it. Bing Crosby is singing on the TV in black and white. I sing along to myself, surprised to find I know all the words. The cushions of this couch are very soft and squishy, and I sink into them, as my eyelids struggle to stay open.

"Did you have a nice time with Jenny today?"

"Jenny?" I look over and see a man sitting next to me. He reaches for my hand—the one without the Band-Aid— and I let him take it. His eyes are kind and familiar, but his face seems pinched with sorrow. He looks a bit like my husband's father, but his voice is low and powerful, just like my husband's. I know he's asked me a question, but I can't—it's not—

"We could get ice cream, if you like," I answer, hoping it makes sense.

"Ice cream?" His eyes open wide but then he smiles. "That's a good idea, Mary. Let's get some ice cream." He helps me off the couch, a movement that seems harder for both of us than it should be.

"Thank me," I say to him, eager to be polite when he struggles so much to help me up.

"Huh?" He looks at me hard, startled maybe. I can't see why, I'm just being nice. "Oh. I get it. You're welcome, Mary." He hugs me and, just for a moment, the love I feel keeps all the confusion away. I'm home, he is my husband, and I am surrounded by love.

PEEPING TOM

No more suspicions, no more denials. I needed to know, once and for all.

The traveling device wasn't accurate, they said, but I had to try. I paid my fee, punched in the date and time, the location. In a flash of light, I was there.

It was his office building, after hours, on that night ten years ago. THE night.

One solitary bulb emitted the only light in the room over his desk. Two shadows, his and hers, played on the darkened wall as I approached, their muffled voices echoing in the silence around them. I crept toward the light, to see and hear for myself what I already knew.

"Come on," she purred, the vile witch. I'd never been able to wipe her face from my memory: the woman who destroyed my marriage. I could imagine her ruby lips pouting in their practiced pose. Fumbling, the sound of lips, a zipper. My heart raced. This was the moment. I would have my proof.

I was surprised how empty my victory felt.

"No," came his voice, quiet but firm. I stopped. Had I been wrong all these years? No. My tiptoes moved toward the sounds of rustling clothing.

"Linda!" He spoke loudly this time, stopping both his ex-wife and soon-to-be-lover in place.

Then he pushed her away and turned down the hall. I ducked into a cubicle as his footsteps approached and the darkness shielded me from his eyes. Tom breezed past, leaving his cologne to caress me one last time. Warm and familiar. I closed my eyes, breathing it in, refusing to admit it held any emotion for me anymore.

Before I could open my eyes, she passed me, following him. I braved a glance after them, just as he rounded on her. His words, a simple sentence that undid the past ten years of my life, stopped her in her tracks: "I love my wife. I would never cheat on her."

ONE FRAYED CORNER

The moment I saw the blanket, I loved it. Mama found it at the bottom of the bin, hidden beneath the donated coats, just one frayed corner sticking out. It was blue and soft, a well-worn square of cotton and wool.

It was also warm. The warmest blanket I'd ever held.

"Here, Chloe," Mama said. "Someone nice wanted you to have this."

I swept the soft fibers across my cheek, happy to have something just for me. The hunger in my belly, the fear in my heart, both disappeared as I clutched the tender cloth to my chin.

"I love it," I whispered, thrilled by the fabric's absorption of my breath. Mama smiled and kissed my forehead, shooing me back to our corner of the shelter.

That night, I slept well, tucked into my fuzzy blue cloud. I was protected from the chilling draft and the other children's muffled sobs as they in fright, clutching clumpy, tear-stained pillows in their fists.   I slept soundly until breakfast.

With my blanket around my shoulders, I savored every bite of my toast and butter and pretended my water was creamy milk. This blanket had enough magic in it to make my whole life better and Mama should know how it felt.

"Mama," I said changing into my other jeans. "You need a blanket too."

"I have one already." She pointed to our cot on the floor and the thin, scratchy blanket on top. With my blanket, I could be warm and happy, maybe even save us from this awful place. Hers was nothing compared to mine; it couldn't even stop her from crying at night.

"That's no good. I'll make you one. You'll see." She smiled kindly, but she didn't believe me, I could tell. I would prove her wrong.

Her blanket should be bigger than mine, so I searched all the donations to gather material: ripped sweaters and scrap fabrics leftover from the unwanted goods of the better-off. One of the volunteers found me a needle and thread just the right size for my small fingers, and I started working.

It took a long time. For days, I worked as long as we had sunshine on our corner. I sent Mama away so she wouldn't see, and then I would hide it beneath the cot. She couldn't see it until it was ready.

When I finished, I stretched the blanket out flat onto the cot. It was so big it folded over once and still fit across! I admired my crooked, misshapen handiwork. My creation wasn't blue and soft, or well-loved like my blanket, but it was warm. The colors and the fabrics didn't match, but I thought it was beautiful.

"For you, Mama. I made it with one frayed corner, just like mine has."

I watched Mama's face closely, as a single tear fell from her eye. She reached out and pulled me against her chest, hugging me tightly. She sniffled once, then said, "It's perfect, sweetheart."

PLUS OR MINUS

They both stared at the clock, waiting for the second hand to make five rotations, one tick at a time, moving around and around in a dizzying circle. Each tick resounded in their chests, in time with their heart beats, and coaxed each breath in and out of their lungs. Their eyes glazed over and lost focus, but neither would blink. Neither would break their gaze on the clock.

Kelly cleared her throat, trying to speak, but only air escaped her lips. Her body stiffened in the uncomfortable silence and she hardened her stare on the clock, daring it to keep ticking. Keeping his eyes ever forward, Peter shifted nervously next to her, making sure not to brush against Kelly as he did so.

Each tick of the clock echoed in the bathroom, bouncing off the four walls before laying the assault against their ears. Each exhaled breath was a wave of sound, swallowing the ticks and cushioning the walls. The tense silence enveloped them both.

Boredom setting in, Kelly stared at her white sneakers, kicking rhythmically at the frayed bathroom rug. She was so entranced that Peter startled her as he shifted his weight on the edge of the bathtub.

"Sorry. Did I scare you?" The silence shattered.

"No, no. I'm just a little dazed right now. This is kinda surreal," she said.

Four minutes to go…

"Yeah, I never thought we be here." He stared at the pregnancy test resting on the sink. "It's weird."

"We haven't given this too much thought."

"Until this morning."

Kelly inhaled deeply. "Peter," she hesitated. "What are we going to do if it's…"

"I don't know. Are we parent material?"

"Guess that doesn't matter much now. It's out of our hands, isn't it?" Kelly moved to the floor and sat cross-legged at Peter's feet.

Chin resting in her hands, her mind reeled. Peter brushed a stray hair from her face, gently tucking it behind her right ear.

"You know, Kelly. This might not be the worst thing that could happen to us."

Kelly straightened, her eyes meeting his for a brief moment. Then, she laughed.

"For a second, I thought you were ser-" His determined gaze stopped her.

"Think about it," he said. "We both have steady jobs with solid incomes, we have been talking about marriage, and we've even discussed getting a puppy…"

"Peter, this is bigger than getting a puppy," she said indignantly. "It doesn't take nine months of your life to birth a puppy, and paper-training is easier than changing diapers."

Three minutes to go…

"All I'm saying is that we're committed to each other already." He took her hands in his as he spoke. "We love each other. We have the means to support a family. It's not like we're sixteen and still in high school."

"But we might be terrible parents." Kelly's words became frantic. "We could seriously mess up this little person. What if he runs away to join the circus because he hates us?" She pulled her hands away from Peter and stood up.

"Kelly, that's ridiculous. Any son of ours will be caring and loving. He'll be smart too. If we plan it correctly, we could even send him to med school. What if he cures cancer?" Peter stood too now, placing his hands gently on Kelly's shoulders. "Won't this conversation seem silly then?"

"My idea is ridiculous? He'd need to get a scholarship if we were ever going to afford med school. He'd better learn to play full symphonies by age three, join every sports team at the high school and become president of the science club," said Kelly, growing more exasperated. "And what if it's a girl?"

Two minutes to go…

"She could be a doctor too, if she wanted, of course." Peter paced the tiny bathroom, excitement in his voice. "Or she could get her MBA and become a big time corporate ball-buster for some Fortune 500 company."

"My daughter will not know the meaning of the words 'power-suit,' thank you very much. She can sing in the choir after school and take ballet lessons until she's good enough to join a touring company, just like I wanted to do when I was fifteen."

"That's the first Commandment about parenting, Kelly: Thou shalt not project thyself onto thy children," he said in his best Charlton Heston voice.

"I'm not projecting! All little girls want to be ballerinas…" she argued, but to no avail. Peter stood motionless, eyebrows raised skeptically. "Fine, forget ballet! What about law school? She could specialize in real estate or tax law, something intelligent yet excessively boring and miles away from any criminals."

"What about the power-suit?"

"If she's a lawyer, she can wear whatever she wants!"

Kelly stole a glance at the clock.

One minute to go…

"Almost there," she sighed, clenching her fists. Tension reclaimed her facial features with every tick.

"What if we had twins?" Peter added. She turned away from the clock and her expression relaxed.

"Twins don't run in my family, so that's unlikely."

"I think they run in mine," he said. "Does that help us?"

"Nope. I don't think I'd want twins any way. Look at me! Twins would obliterate me and eight-minute abs."

Peter laughed. "We could probably only handle one for now anyway. I don't think I'd know the front of a diaper from the back, you know?"

Silence set in again. Could we even handle one? The unspoken question lingered in the air between them like heavy steam after a long shower.

"We're old enough," said Kelly.

"Right."

"And we love each other."

"Of course."

"We might even buy a house this year."

"Just as I said, we'll be fine." Peter reached for her again, but Kelly slipped through his arms, lost in thought.

"And if we can get him or her into a good private school, we might have a chance at a scholarship. I mean, we both had decent grades in school..." Kelly stopped when she caught Peter's furrowed brow. "What? What's wrong?"

"Well, don't you think it's unfair to assume that our child will want to go to private school? I didn't, and I still got a scholarship to Stanford," Peter said pointedly.

"I'm just saying that his or her chances would be better if…"

"If we throw a bunch of money at some expensive school?" he interrupted.

"That's not what I meant. Anyhow, we can discuss that in thirteen years when the time comes to decide." Kelly wasn't interested in starting an argument when the tension level was already so high.

"Exactly. And I believe our child should have a say."

"Well at least he can play soccer wherever he goes," she said. "Look, only fifteen more seconds. Are you nervous?"

"What? Yes, of course. But soccer, Kel? Really?" He grabbed her hand as she reached for the pregnancy test. "Wait just one minute."

"We've just waited the five longest minutes of my life," Kelly said, her voice edged with panic. "In ten seconds, this conversation might not be necessary."

"Who cares if it's necessary now? We're going to need to have the conversation at some point."

"So that's a no to playing soccer, huh?"

"We can discuss baseball, football or track. No soccer," he spoke vehemently.

"Any particular reason?"

"Because those are the sports that I played when I was in high school, and I could coach the pee-wee teams. So, that's what my son will play." He crossed his arms and stared at her.

"Now who's projecting?" Kelly laughed at his stubborn glower. "Come on, time's up. I can't take it anymore. I have to know."

"Ok, fine. Take a deep breath and go."

Without looking, Kelly snatched the test from the tooth-paste stained sink. She perched uncomfortably on the narrow rim of the tub, next to Peter. Clutching the stick, her knuckles equally as white, Kelly turned to Peter and held out her hand.

"I can't look. You have to do it." She opened her fist and offered it to him, her eyes squeezed tightly closed.

Peter hesitated. His hand shook as he took the pregnancy test from Kelly's clammy palm. With a deep breath he turned it towards him and read the results.

"Well..."

ABOUT THE AUTHOR

Stephanie Haddad's earliest works featured unicorns and talking pumpkins who overcame adversity, evil, and the threat of being baked into pies. With age, her writing has evolved to more grown-up topics, like love and the complicated relationships between people. As a life-long lover of cheerful fiction, she strives to tackle real-world issues with wit, hope, and lots of humor. Her short stories have spanned many genres, but her full-length novels stay firmly planted in happy endings. Combining a passion for the human condition with a penchant for the romantic, Stephanie strives to write every story as though it is a conversation shared between friends.

She is the author of four romance novels: *A Previous Engagement, Love Regifted, Love Unlisted,* and *Socially Awkward.* She lives, loves, and writes near Boston, MA, the home of all of her novels.

Visit www.stephaniehaddad.com for more information on Stephanie's forthcoming work.

Made in United States
North Haven, CT
14 July 2022

21311810R00033